My "q" Sound Box®

Library of Congress Cataloging-in-Publication Data
Moncure, Jane Belk.
My "q" sound box / by Jane Belk Moncure; illustrated by Colin King.
p. cm.
Summary: A little girl fills her sound box with many words beginning with the letter "q."
ISBN 1-56766-783-X
[1. Alphabet.] I. King, Colin, ill. II. Title.
PZ7.M739 Myq   2000
[E]—dc21   99-054326

My "q"
Sound Box®

Jane Belk Moncure

illustrated by Colin King

The
Child's
World®

Little  had a box.

"I will find things that begin with my 'q' sound," she said.

"I will put them into my sound box."

Little

found quilts . . .

quite a lot of quilts.

Two quails watched her quietly.

Little q folded the quilts,

and filled her box with quilts.

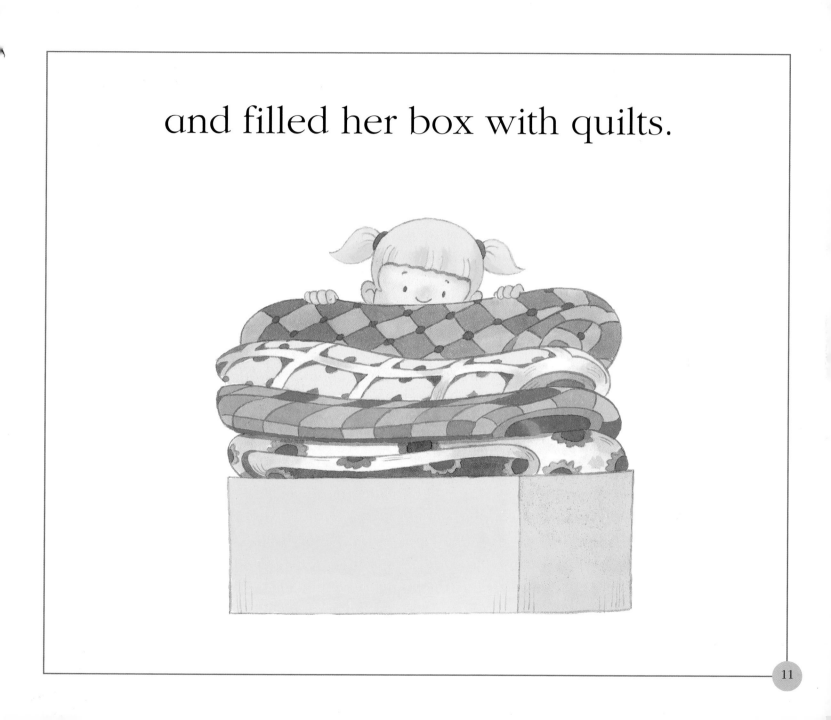

There was one quilt left.

Little q wrapped the quilt around herself.

"I can be a queen," she said.

Just then, Little  met a real queen.

"If you want to look like a real queen, you must have a crown," said the queen.

So Little  found some

quarters . . .

quite a lot of quarters.

She counted her quarters.
How many did she have?

Little q took the quarters

to the store.

Little q bought a crown.

The two queens played until
they were hungry.

Little  q found a quart of milk

and a quart of quince jam.

Then she and the queen
ate lunch.

Little q put what

was left into the box.

Then Little  q said, "It's late!
Let's go to bed."

"No! No!" said the queen.

"A real queen must have a queen's bed."

Little q looked for more quarters

so that she could buy a queen's bed.
She looked and looked. But she could
not find any more quarters.

Then Little  saw her box with all the quilts inside.

"I will turn my box into a queen's bed," she said.

Little  put a quilt on top of the box.

"Now let's go to bed," she said.
She jumped into the box.

"No! No! No!" said the real queen.

So they quarreled and quarreled . . .

until  quarter past nine.

Then the real queen was
so tired of quarreling
that she quit!

So she jumped
into the box with Little
They pulled up the
quilts and went to sleep.

Can you read these words with Little q?

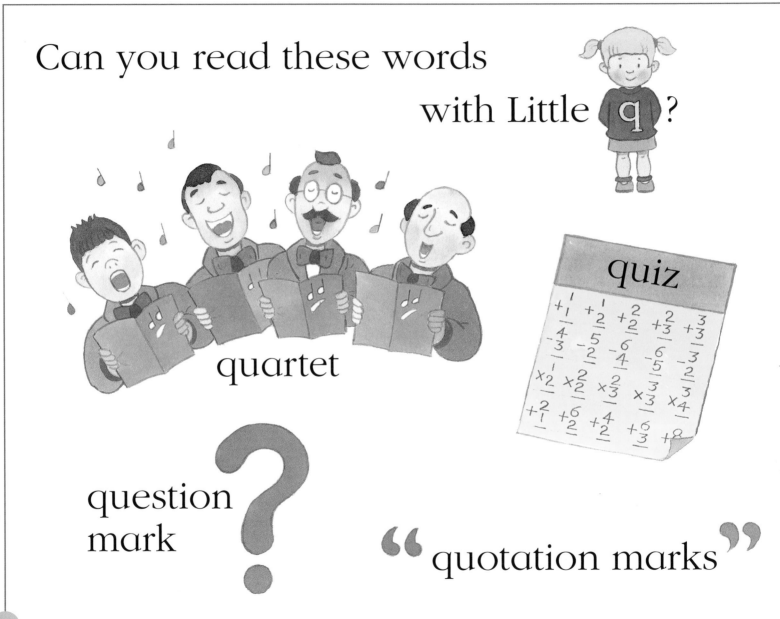

quartet

quiz

question mark

"quotation marks"

quills

Quaker

quintuplets

quince

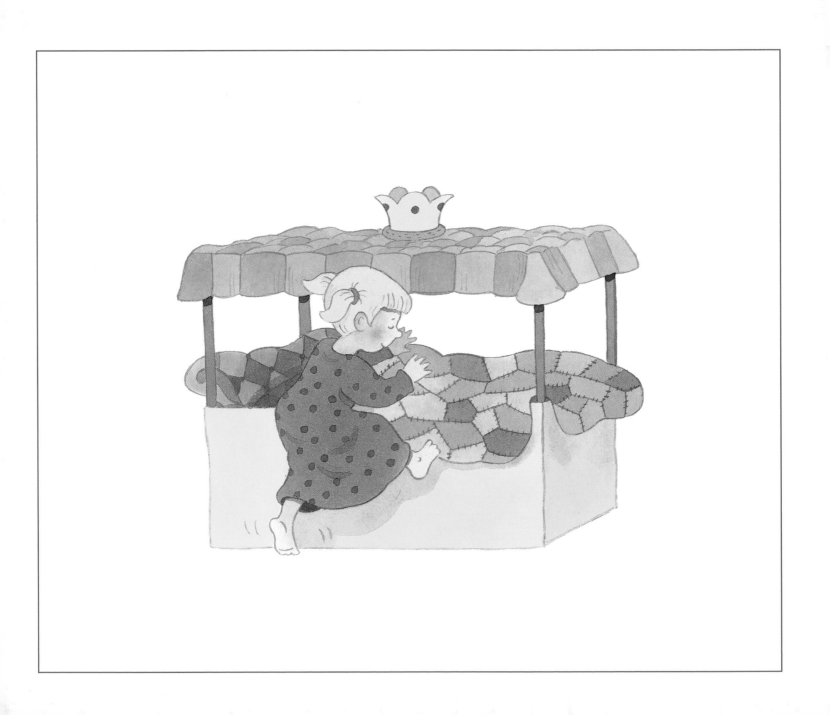

ABOUT THE AUTHOR AND ILLUSTRATOR

Jane Belk Moncure began her writing career when she was in kindergarten. She has never stopped writing. Many of her children's stories and poems have been published, to the delight of young readers, including her son Jim, whose childhood experiences found their way into many of her books.

Mrs. Moncure's writing is based upon an active career in early childhood education. A recipient of an M.A. degree from Columbia University, Mrs. Moncure has taught and directed nursery, kindergarten, and primary grade programs in California, New York, Virginia, and North Carolina. As a former member of the faculties of Virginia Commonwealth University and the University of Richmond, she taught prospective teachers in early childhood education.

Mrs. Moncure has travelled extensively abroad, studying early childhood programs in the United Kingdom, The Netherlands, and Switzerland. She was the first president of the Virginia Association for Early Childhood Education and received its award for outstanding service to young children.

A resident of North Carolina, Mrs. Moncure is currently a full-time writer and educational consultant. She is married to Dr. James A. Moncure, former vice president of Elon College.

Colin King studied at the Royal College of Art, London. He started his freelance career as an illustrator, working for magazines and advertising agencies.

He began drawing pictures for children's books in 1976 and has illustrated over sixty titles to date.

Included in a wide variety of subjects are a best-selling children's encyclopedia and books about spies and detectives.

His books have been translated into several languages, including Japanese and Hebrew. He has four grown-up children and lives in Suffolk, England, with his wife, three dogs, and a cat.